P9-ELI-548

Blue's Thanksgiving Feast

by Jessica Lissy

illustrated by David Cutting

Simon Spotlight/Nick Jr.

New York   London   Toronto   Sydney   Singapore

For my amazing family—Mom, Dad, Micah, and Rachel—with love
and thanks for all their help.—J. L.

For my Aunt and Uncle—Mary (Tiny) and Paul Colandrea—who made every
occasion to be with them a Holiday!—D. C.

Note to Parents from Creators: In *Blue's Thanksgiving Feast*, everyone is
working to create a special holiday meal. Blue and her friends need your
child's help to prepare food, set the table, and make decorations for their
Thanksgiving feast. Along the way, this book encourages your child to think
about cooperating and working together on a project, while also providing a
chance to build visual perception, counting, and math skills. We hope that reading
Blue's Thanksgiving Feast will inspire you and your child to talk about how friends share
and help one another.

Based on the TV series *Blue's Clues*® created by Traci Paige Johnson, Todd Kessler, and
Angela C. Santomero as seen on Nick Jr.® On *Blue's Clues*, Steve is played by Steven Burns.

SIMON SPOTLIGHT
An imprint of Simon & Schuster Children's Publishing Division
1230 Avenue of the Americas New York, New York 10020 Copyright © 2001 Viacom International Inc. All rights reserved.
NICKELODEON, NICK JR., *Blue's Clues*, and all related titles, logos, and characters are trademarks of Viacom International Inc.
All rights reserved including the right of reproduction in whole or in part in any form. SIMON SPOTLIGHT and colophon are
registered trademarks of Simon & Schuster.
Manufactured in the United States of America
First Edition   10 9 8 7 6 5 4 3 2
ISBN 0-689-84185-X

Hi! We're having a special Thanksgiving feast today. And since you're such a special friend, Blue and I want you to come. Will you help us get ready? Great! Let's go to the backyard.

Everyone is working hard to get ready for the feast. Shovel and Pail are picking vegetables for Mr. Salt and Mrs. Pepper to cook.

Can you help
us find everything
on this list?

Can you
guess what food
Mr. Salt is going to make
with the pumpkins
we picked?

Look at all the vegetables we picked together!

Do you see anyone else working together to find food?

The kitchen smells good! Here's our list for the Thanksgiving stuffing. Will you help Mr. Salt, Mrs. Pepper, and Paprika find the ingredients? Thanks!

Mr. Salt already has the vegetables you picked. Can you find everything else he needs?

Next, Mrs. Pepper needs the biggest pot and the longest spoon. Can you help Mr. Salt and Paprika find them?

Will you help Mr. Salt and Paprika find a lid that matches the pot too?

Thanks for helping with the stuffing! You're a great Thanksgiving cook! What do we need to do next, Blue?

Help get the table ready, of course! Blue wants to set up eight chairs for our friends. How many more does she need?

You're right, three more chairs, thanks! Now will you help Slippery and Tickety set the table so it's ready for our Thanksgiving feast?

Oh, Blue wants to make turkey placecards so our friends will know where to sit. She's making a card for Slippery. Can you help Blue find a pink letter *S* for Slippery?

Thanks for your help!

Now we just need to find our Thankful Book. Can you help us find it? Then we can add the things we're thankful for this year. What are you thankful for?

Our friends out here are collecting decorations. Can you help Blue gather pinecones to decorate our Thanksgiving table?

Blue also wants big, red leaves. How many do you see?

You found our decorations. Thanks! But where did Blue go?

Have a seat! Can you find all the things you helped us do?
Thanks so much for helping us with our special feast!
Happy Thanksgiving!